# DISASTER STRIKES

## Tornado Alley

# DON'T MISS A MINUTE OF THESE HEART-STOPPING ADVENTURES!

## Earthquake Shock

## Tornado Alley

# DISASTER STRIKES

## Tornado Alley

by **MARLANE KENNEDY**

illustrated by
**ERWIN MADRID**

SCHOLASTIC INC.

For my friend Michelle Houts, who writes children's books and happily lives on a farm with cattle, goats, and a much adored Great Pyrenees mountain dog.

ISBN 978-0-545-53046-0

12 11 10 9 8 7 6 5 4 3 2          14 15 16 17 18 19/0

Printed in the U.S.A.    40
First printing, April 2014

Designed by Nina Goffi

# CHAPTER 1

Wyatt Anderson came into the kitchen, holding a tub of squiggling worms he'd just dug up. Soon his best buddies, Joshua and Jackson Petree, would be arriving. They would be saddling up the horses, riding over to the pond, and fishing. Wyatt couldn't wait!

Jackson was Wyatt's age, ten, and Joshua was nine. They went to the same school as Wyatt and played on his football team. The Petrees lived on the next ranch over, which was about seven miles away. Out in their part of Oklahoma, there was no such thing as a close neighbor!

Wyatt's mother hunched over the counter, scribbling a shopping list to get ready for her trip into town. His father had loaded the pickup truck with tools and had gone to mend a fence in the east pasture. The Andersons had a large cattle ranch with about eight hundred head of cattle. Usually, Wyatt loved helping out at the ranch, especially moving and sorting cattle. But mending fence was pretty boring, so he was glad his father had given him the day off — in honor of the first day of summer vacation, and also because his cousin, Alison, had just arrived from New York City for a stay.

Mrs. Anderson looked up from her list. "Where is Alison?" she asked Wyatt.

"Out in the barn with Duncan," Wyatt said.

"Duncan is not supposed to be entertaining Alison. You are!" his mother scolded.

Wyatt just rolled his eyes. He didn't want to entertain Alison. She was annoying. His aunt and uncle had adopted her from Korea when she was two, and the cousins didn't see each other that often so he didn't really know her all that well. But he wasn't impressed by what he did know. She was giggly. She was a ballerina. She liked pink everything. They had nothing in common.

To remedy the situation, Wyatt's mother and his aunt, Alison's mom, came up with the idea of a cousin swap. Alison would spend two weeks at the beginning of summer on the ranch. Then the last two weeks of summer, Wyatt would go stay with Alison and her family in New York City. The grown-ups thought it would "expand their horizons." But to Wyatt it was just plain stupid. Alison would ruin his first moments of summer fun on the ranch. And spending two weeks in a high-rise apartment cooped up with Alison sounded like torture.

His mother frowned at him. Wyatt could tell she was not pleased with his attitude.

"I can't help it if Alison is crazy about Duncan and wants to spend all her time in the barn with him!" Wyatt protested.

Duncan was the Anderson's big white Great Pyrenees mountain dog. He spent most of his time in and around the barn closest to the house. The barn and the fenced-in areas to the side and behind it were home to the horses and Mrs. Anderson's small herd of pygmy goats. Duncan had an important job. He acted as companion and guardian to the animals, especially the tiny goats, protecting them from coyotes, mountain lions, and bobcats.

Wyatt heard the sound of a car pulling up, and soon Joshua and Jackson appeared by the back screen door.

"Come on in, boys," Mrs. Anderson said.

Both of the Petree boys, with their dark hair and dark eyes, took after their mother, whose ancestors were members of the Choctaw tribe. But other than that, the boys were very different. Jackson was tall and thin with longish hair that hung in his eyes, while Joshua was short and stocky with a buzz cut. Jackson was the responsible one and Joshua was impulsive. The two boys grinned at Wyatt, and then Joshua immediately ran for the cookie jar that Mrs. Anderson always kept stocked with freshly baked chocolate chip cookies. He grabbed two and stuffed one in his mouth.

"Joshua!" Jackson said, trying to remind his brother of his manners.

"Go ahead and help yourself, Joshua —
and you, too, Jackson!" Mrs. Anderson
laughed. She really didn't mind. The Petree
brothers were like family.

Wyatt held out the tub of worms while
Jackson and Joshua munched on the home-
made cookies. "Got some nice ones!" he
said. "Let's get the horses ready and head
on over to the pond."

"Take your cell phone with you," Mrs. Anderson reminded Wyatt. "And be sure to saddle up a horse for Alison so she can go with you!"

Wyatt grabbed his phone off the counter and shoved it in his back pocket. "Alison doesn't know how to ride a horse." He scoffed. "She can't come."

"Give her Molasses. He's old and steady. If a person can sit, they can ride Molasses," Mrs. Anderson replied, smiling.

Wyatt tried another approach. "You should take her to town with you, Mom. She'd probably rather go shopping."

"I'm going to the grocery store. Not anywhere exciting," his mother said, shaking her head. "I told my sister we would give Alison the full ranch experience. Now take the boys out to the barn and introduce them to Alison. Shoo!" Mrs. Anderson waved them off.

When the three boys got to the barn, they found Alison hugging on Duncan, his tail wagging, a big slobbery smile on his face. Then Wyatt noticed something that mortified him. Alison had tied two pink ribbons around Duncan's ears! Joshua and Jackson started cracking up at the sight.

"You've robbed him of all his dignity!" Wyatt cried.

Alison just giggled and stood up. And that's when he got a good look at the lettering on her shirt. Underneath a picture of a pair of pointe shoes, it said *If ballet was easy, they would call it football*.

Wyatt cringed. "This is my cousin, Alison," he said, without much enthusiasm. Maybe Joshua and Jackson would come up with some kind of wisecrack about her shirt. They would put her in her place!

But Joshua just smiled and said, "Funny shirt!" Like he was complimenting her or something. Jackson just stared at her in a dopey, love-struck way. Like he liked her. Like he *liked her* liked her. Good grief!

Wyatt had to admit his cousin was pretty, with her long, silky black hair and a wide smile with perfect teeth. But he felt like his buddies had betrayed him. Maybe it wasn't fair, but part of him wanted them to give her the cold shoulder, too.

The trip to the pond should have taken fifteen minutes, but the time felt doubled because of old slowpoke Molasses. He got his name because of his deep-brown color, though now that he was getting older, the name was especially fitting. He used to work the ranch, but these days he was mostly retired.

Wyatt rode his very own horse, Licorice, who was tall, with a shiny black coat, and quick as lightning. He could cut cattle like nobody's business! Wyatt and Licorice had even won a collection of barrel-racing trophies, but now they had to plod along because of Alison and Molasses. Beside them Joshua sat astride Cream Puff, Mr. Anderson's handsome palomino, and Jackson rode flashy S'more, a black-and-white-spotted horse that belonged to Wyatt's mother. The Andersons had a tradition of naming their horses after sweet treats.

Duncan dutifully trailed behind the horses. Without the pink ribbons. It was daylight and the goats were safe, but he seemed to think Alison was a new charge that needed looking after.

Alison chatted nonstop the whole way. Mostly about how lucky Wyatt was to have so many animals around. "I want a dog so bad," she said. She looked at Duncan wistfully. "But our apartment building doesn't allow them."

As they neared the pond Alison broke out in song, belting off-key at the top of her lungs. "Yippi ti yi yo, get along little doggies . . ."

Wyatt didn't know whether to be embarrassed or annoyed. But soon Joshua and Jackson joined right in, singing the song, too. Wyatt let out an exasperated sigh, but he grudgingly added his voice to the mix, not wanting to be left out.

They finally reached the pond and tied the horses under the shade of a few nearby trees. Wyatt squinted, staring off in the distance, not happy with what he saw. Miles and miles away, angry dark clouds were rolling across the sky. "We'd better hurry up and get our fishing in," he told everyone. "Looks like we're going to be chased off by a bad storm before too long."

# CHAPTER 2

The kids grabbed their fishing equipment and made their way to the edge of the pond. Wyatt looked down at the tub of worms, and suddenly a really funny idea popped into his head. He lifted the lid and shoved it under Alison's nose, hoping to give her a good scare. It'd serve her right for spoiling the beginning of summer for him.

But instead of screaming or shrieking, Alison stuck her hand in the tub and picked up one of the wiggling worms. "Hey there, Mr. Worm," she said. "You're kind of cute!"

Joshua and Jackson laughed, which aggravated Wyatt to no end. He could tell how much they liked Alison. Whose side were they on anyway?

When Alison announced the worm was way too cute for her to put on her hook, Jackson gallantly volunteered. "I'll do it for you," he said, carefully threading the worm through the hook.

Joshua abruptly shoved his brother out of the way and squeezed in beside Alison, grabbing her pole. "Let me show you how to cast your line so the bobber ends up in the middle of the pond."

While his friends fussed over Alison, Wyatt just busied himself with his own pole, hoping to catch the first fish of the day.

As the four sat on the bank watching their bobbers, Duncan came over and laid his head in Alison's lap. She stroked his head and mumbled sweet nothings to him, leaning over so their noses almost touched. "Such a sweet boy. You're a good old dog, aren't you?"

After an hour Joshua had caught two fish and Jackson one. Wyatt had caught four. His last one was the largest catch of the day. He was the only one who was taking fishing seriously. Joshua and Jackson were too busy asking Alison all about New York City.

"Have you been to the top of the Empire State Building?" Jackson asked.

"Have you ever been mugged?" Joshua interrupted, before she could answer.

"Yes to the first question and no to the second, thank goodness!" Alison laughed. "Really, I feel very safe where I live."

Wyatt just tried to tune them out.

Silly Alison hadn't caught any fish. Her line would bob, but she would reel it in too late — only to find the fish had eaten the worm right off her hook. She kept looking down at Duncan and fussed over him instead of minding her pole.

The dark clouds were getting closer. A crack of lightning flashed far off in the distance. "We'd better get going," Wyatt said.

"Hey, I've got something!" Alison suddenly shouted. She reeled in her line and there, flipping around, was a huge bass. Bigger than anything Wyatt had caught. "I can't believe I caught one," Alison said gleefully.

"Oh, man! It's a beaut!" said Joshua.

"Not bad for a first timer," added Jackson.

"I said we need to get going!" Wyatt said more forcefully. "The storm coming in looks bad!"

"Awww, it's still sunny right now," Jackson said. "We have time. No need to rush."

Duncan started to whimper. He headed for the horses, then turned around and gave everyone a quizzical look.

"I think he wants to get back to the goats," Alison said. "Maybe we should head home."

Wyatt should have felt grateful that Alison was agreeing with him. But when he looked at the ominous clouds, all he saw was a dark mirror of his mood. Plus, with Molasses slowing them down, they'd be lucky to make it back before the rain hit.

The angry darkness chased the kids as they rode back to the barn. Wyatt kept looking over his shoulder. There was something different about this storm. The clouds marched in a tall tower that was at least a couple of miles high. And they were tinged an eerie green. Thunder sounded in the distance. But oddly, as they approached the barn, the sun was still shining brightly.

By the time they got within a hundred feet of the barn, rain cut loose from the heavy cloud wall and began to pelt them. Each drop stung Wyatt's face. Alison shrieked like it was great fun riding in the rain. An adventure. Joshua and Jackson laughed, too. But Wyatt didn't appreciate getting soaked to the bone. The air had turned cold, and as the wind started to pick up, he shivered and hustled toward the barn, where he jumped off Licorice and opened the door, letting everyone inside.

They took the tack off the horses and put their gear away, then rubbed and brushed the horses down before leading them into their stalls. Duncan trotted off to check on his goats, with Alison close behind. She climbed into the pen, scratched the mama goat under her chin, then picked up one of her tiny week-old triplet babies and nuzzled it with her cheek. "You are sooooo sweet," she said. "I wish I could take you home with me."

Duncan barked.

"Oh, and you, too, Duncan!" Alison laughed. "I would probably have better luck bringing a pygmy goat into the apartment than Duncan," she called to the boys. "I can't believe how small these goats are. Even the mama. Duncan is way bigger!

Just as Joshua and Jackson were about to climb into the goat pen with Alison, Wyatt turned to them and frowned.

"We should go inside," he said. He wanted to change into some dry clothes and play video games with Joshua and Jackson before they had to go home. But all at once an ear-shattering clatter shook the metal roof of the barn.

The kids all jumped in surprise.

*Hail?* Wyatt wondered. He peeked out the barn door while the others scrambled over the rails of the goat pen after him. Hailstones about the size of golf balls bounced off the ground.

"Holy cow!" Jackson said.

"Oh my gosh!" Alison stood with her mouth gaping open.

Joshua stuck his hand outside, like he wanted to catch a piece of hail. Jackson quickly pulled his younger brother back. "Don't be stupid. That hail is big enough to hurt you!"

Then just as suddenly as the hail started, it stopped.

"Man, that was weird!" Joshua said.

"It was. But it's over now, so let's head for the house," Wyatt said. "I need to beat you guys at *FreakFighters*!"

"I love that game!" cried Alison. "And I'm pretty good at it, too!"

Wyatt looked at her like she was crazy. How could she think he'd been talking to her? Like a ballerina could beat him at *FreakFighters*. Yeah, right.

As the kids walked toward the house, the air felt oddly still. Quiet. It was unsettling.

Especially after the driving rain and hail they'd just experienced.

Wyatt looked westward, the direction the storm had come from, and saw something so surreal and terrifying on the horizon that he had to do a double take to make sure his eyes weren't deceiving him. For a moment he stood absolutely still, awestruck by the enormous funnel cloud that kicked up swirling columns of dust in the distance. There was something hypnotizing about it. Part of Wyatt wanted to stand there and watch, but soon his common sense took over.

"Tornado!" Wyatt screamed. "Get to the storm shelter!" He pointed at the cellar doors by the side of the house. "We have to get to shelter. Run!"

For a split second, the others froze in their tracks, startled by Wyatt's outburst, until they, too, saw the tornado. The wind picked up and whipped around them, pushing away the stillness, and all four kids bolted, making a beeline for safety.

Wyatt was surprised to see Alison outrun them all. She was fast and reached the cellar doors first, quickly followed by long-legged Jackson. They heaved open the doors, revealing a staircase down to the cellar, and paused for a moment, waiting for Wyatt and Joshua to catch up.

"Don't wait. Get inside!" Wyatt yelled.

Jackson and Alison obeyed his command and disappeared down the steps, with Joshua scrambling in close behind them. *Phew! We're all safe,* Wyatt thought as he darted down the first few steps and reached to close the doors. But before he could get a hold of them, a flash of pink streaked by.

"Duncan is in the barn," Alison shouted as she rushed back up the steps. "I have to go get him and bring him to the cellar!"

"Are you nuts? Get back here!" Wyatt lunged for her, but she slipped out of his grasp. "There's no time!" he yelled after her with desperation and fury in his voice.

Alison turned and looked at him briefly with panicked eyes. The wind flung her long dark hair every which way. And then in an instant she was gone. Running away from them. Away from safety.

And into the path of a monster.

# CHAPTER 3

"Stay here!" Wyatt called down to Joshua and Jackson. "I'll be right back." Then, without thinking, Wyatt went after his cousin, running as fast as his feet could carry him. By now the wind was howling. The tornado was bearing down. In a matter of minutes, it'd gotten dangerously close, and a veil of dirt stung his eyes.

"Alison!" he screamed into the wind.

But she didn't seem to hear him. The distance between them grew larger. Alison's legs were strong from ballet, and they carried her through the gusts of wind that kept knocking Wyatt off course. He fought back, zigging and zagging his way after her, too afraid to glance to the side to see where the tornado was.

He sensed the presence of something hurtling through the air toward him and instinctively raised his arms for protection. The flying tree branch that rushed past barely missed him, coming within inches of knocking him in the side of his head.

*Don't let anything happen to my family,* thought Wyatt. *Even Alison. If the tornado will just change course, I'll be nicer to her, I swear.* How much time did he have left to save her? A few minutes? Seconds? Soon it would be too late.

He couldn't even see her any longer. She must have darted inside the barn. *But that's not any safer than being outside,* Wyatt couldn't help thinking. *We need to get back to the storm cellar!*

A few more strides later, Wyatt burst through the barn door to find Alison pulling Duncan by his collar.

It was then that Wyatt heard a noise like a freight train barreling toward them. And soon the barn began to shake.

"We have to find something to cover us!" Wyatt shouted. "Something big and heavy. The tornado's about to hit!"

"But we have to get back to the cellar!" Alison protested, her eyes wide with fear.

"There's no time!" Wyatt looked around for anything that could offer protection. In the aisle of the barn, near some stacks of hay, he spotted a garden tractor with a small utility trailer hitched behind it. "Under there!" He grabbed Alison by the elbow and shoved her toward the trailer.

Alison took a flying leap toward the trailer, rolling underneath. "Duncan, come here, boy. Come here!" She pounded the ground, pleading. Duncan crawled under with her. The barn began to creak and groan. Wyatt took a quick look out the open barn door. The sky was dark, as if night had suddenly fallen. He flung himself under the trailer, too.

Wyatt didn't know how the churning, rumbling noise could grow any louder, but it did. Spooky whistling filled the air. Farm tools crashed and pounded against the walls of the barn. They were under attack.

On Alison's side, bales of hay buffered her from the chaos, but Duncan couldn't stop panting and whimpering from where he lay between the cousins. One of the goats nervously bleated a low *maaaaaaa*, reminding Wyatt that the other animals weren't as protected as Duncan. Licorice's stall was across the aisle and Wyatt heard his shrill neigh, his frenzied kicking against the walls of his stall.

"Whoa, boy! Whoa!" Wyatt called out, trying to calm Licorice. He was frightened that his horse would end up hurting himself.

But Licorice could not be calmed — the kicking continued until a crack and a crashing boomed over the ruckus of the storm. Wyatt listened helplessly to the sound of thundering hooves as his horse fled from the barn.

How soon would the twister be on top of them, ripping everything in Wyatt's life apart? Each second secmed like an eternity.

"I'm sorry!" Alison yelled in an effort to be heard above the noise. "I shouldn't have left the cellar. I was just worried about Duncan, but I should have listened to you."

Wyatt wanted to scold her, but she looked so helpless and scared. He started to tell her it was okay when a section of the roof suddenly ripped from the barn walls with an explosive *whoosh*. Feed buckets, saddles, bridles, and bales of hay tumbled around them. Alison went silent, and Wyatt knew apologies didn't matter anymore. None of it mattered. The tornado was here and there was nothing that could be done about it. The trailer they were hiding under clanked and pinged as items small and large pelted it from every side.

A moment later a giant arm of pressure grasped at Wyatt. He clung to the edge of the undercarriage in a desperate attempt to keep from being sucked out from under the trailer.

"I've got you!" Alison reached over Duncan, wrapping her arms around her cousin's neck.

Wyatt instantly knew that was a mistake. She would be sucked into the tornado along with him. "Let go!" he said.

"I won't! Wrap your legs around the rod connecting the wheels. That's what I'm doing!" Alison screamed in his ear.

Wyatt felt around for the axle and looped a leg over it, crossing his ankles as a powerful gust picked up the trailer, along with Alison and Wyatt. They were hovering above the ground!

He clung to the trailer, but felt himself slipping. Stubborn Alison refused to let go of his neck. Wyatt could barely breathe as he watched the trailer hitch give way and break loose from the tractor.

They were flying, and then, with a sudden jolt, the trailer dropped to the ground just as the awful churning noise of the freight train died. Wyatt and Alison stared at each other for a moment, the air knocked from their lungs, both too stunned to speak. Alison still had him in a death grip.

"I think you can let go of me now," Wyatt finally said.

Alison gave a sheepish grin, which quickly faded when she noticed the empty space between them. "Duncan!" she gasped. "What happened to Duncan!"

# CHAPTER 4

Wyatt and Alison scampered out from under the trailer, looking around in shock at the devastation that met them. A big patch of roof had indeed been ripped completely off the barn. The family's two four-wheelers had been flipped onto their sides, a good thirty feet away from where they'd been parked. Bales of hay and straw lay busted and strewn, creating a spotty carpet of gold and green. The air was dusty and thick. A pitchfork speared the top of one of the horse stall doors, as if a giant had hurled it at the beasts and missed, striking wood instead. Molasses stuck his head above the door, with big dazed eyes. He snorted. Cream Puff and S'more made their presence known, too, whinnying to each other.

"Where's Licorice?" Alison asked.

"Gone," Wyatt said. "I heard him kick down his door right before the tornado struck." The enormity of what had just happened suddenly hit Wyatt now that the immediate danger of the tornado was gone. Memories of barrel races and cutting cattle on top of his trusty friend flooded his mind. Wyatt took a ragged breath. His cheeks felt hot. Licorice was fast and he could turn on a dime. *Could he have made it?* Wyatt clung to hope, but still a sense of grief poured through him.

Alison began to cry, mumbling something about Duncan and Licorice, but she quickly pulled herself together and looked at her cousin. "I'm so glad you're okay, Wyatt. I almost got you killed."

Wyatt didn't feel in the mood to hold a grudge. Too much had happened. "You held on to me. You saved me," he said. "We're both here, despite the tornado, and we should focus on that. Let's go find Joshua and Jackson and make sure they're okay, too."

As Wyatt and Alison made their way out

of the barn, picking through the once neat and now littered aisle, they passed the spot where the trailer had been. The nearby bales of hay were no longer stacked in orderly rows. Some had blown away, while others remained in jumbled disarray.

In a small nook created by some of the bales, a flash of white fur could be seen.

"Duncan!" Alison shouted.

The excited dog crawled out and ran over to her. She dropped to her knees and hugged him tightly as he licked her face in greeting. Wyatt bent over and patted Duncan on the head, glad to see his old friend, too.

But soon Duncan broke away from Alison and ran over to the goat pens. He needed to check on his little herd. Wyatt and Alison followed him.

The metal pens were mangled and the goats were huddled together near the wall. Duncan sniffed each one until he'd made sure they were all okay. Wyatt and Alison left him in charge and stepped outside.

*Whew!* Wyatt let out a big sigh of relief at the sight of his house. It was still standing, though many of the windows were shattered and the front porch was pretty much gone. Only two walls of the detached garage still stood. The rest had been completely destroyed. Wyatt knew how much worse it could have been. But once he saw the storm cellar doors at the side of the house, his heart sank. They were wide open.

Did that mean Joshua and Jackson didn't stay inside like he told them to and instead tried to follow them to the barn? Had they been caught in the tornado, swept away?

Wyatt was about to panic when the two brothers appeared from behind the remaining walls of the detached garage. They ran up to Wyatt and Alison, relief pulling at the corners of their eyes.

"Oh gosh, we thought you guys were goners! We were just heading to the barn to look for you," Joshua said breathlessly.

"When the tornado hit, we heard crazy noises from inside the cellar," Jackson added. "It sounded like the whole farm was just obliterated, and we were scared something bad had happened to you!"

"We were in the barn, hiding under a trailer," Wyatt explained. "Thank goodness the barn didn't collapse or we actually would have been goners." Now that he and his friends had found one another he looked off into the distance to take stock of the situation. He saw dark skies, a flash of lightning, but no funnel cloud.

Jackson looked around, too, brushing

back his long hair from his eyes. "The tornado. There's no sign of it. It must have dissipated."

But Wyatt knew his father had gone out to the east pasture to mend fence — which was the direction the tornado had been heading.

It dawned on Wyatt that he had his cell phone in his back pocket. He quickly took it out and punched in his father's number, but he got no answer. The line didn't even ring. "Can't reach my dad," he told the others. "The tornado must have taken out the nearest cell phone tower. I need to go find him. Make sure he is okay." It would take forever to walk out there, but the two four-wheelers in the barn had looked okay even though they'd tipped. If even one of them was still functional, maybe he could ride it out to the east pasture.

It took some muscle, but eventually the four kids were able to lift both four-wheelers upright. The keys still dangled from the ignition, and though the frames were a little bent, each one started just fine. Wyatt thought he'd be going by himself, but everyone insisted on joining him in case Mr. Anderson was in some sort of trouble, so he relented.

"Alison, you can ride with me," Wyatt said as climbed aboard one and motioned behind him.

"Okay," she said nervously as she hopped on and grabbed him tightly around the waist. "I've never ridden on one of these things."

"If you can manage to cling to a trailer in a tornado, this'll be a piece of cake." Wyatt couldn't help but grin.

Joshua and Jackson climbed aboard the other four-wheeler, and soon the group was easing their way around the debris that littered the yard. Once they were out in the open, Wyatt gunned it.

It was a fast, bumpy ride, but Wyatt was in a hurry to check on his dad. They slowed down briefly to weave around some cattle and later to splash through a creek bed, the water soaking their legs. But when they were in open pasture, Wyatt kept his head down and his focus clear — he was going full throttle all the way.

After about fifteen minutes, Wyatt saw his dad's white pickup truck headed their way. He was okay! His dad was okay!

All at once he noticed Joshua and Jackson weren't racing beside him on their four-wheeler. He thought he heard one of them shout. Wyatt slowed to a stop and glanced backward.

The other four-wheeler was parked a dozen yards back. Jackson sat paralyzed, looking up at the sky, his face as pale as if he had seen a ghost.

Wyatt tilted his head up in the direction Jackson was looking, and his jaw dropped. A wide patch of clouds swirled between the four-wheelers and his father's approaching truck. A wisp of smoky white spun and quickly inched its way down, stretching toward the ground like a great reaching hand. Wyatt didn't know whether to feel terror or astonishment. A second tornado was forming right before his very eyes. It was happening again. He sat on the four-wheeler, spellbound by the strangely majestic sight.

"Wyatt," Alison whispered. "What are we going to do?"

Wyatt didn't know what to say. They were in the middle of miles of open range. This time, there was nowhere for them to go. Nowhere for them to hide.

# CHAPTER 5

Within seconds the tornado had hit the ground, darkening the area where the narrow bottom of the funnel touched down. It was only about a half mile away, Wyatt figured, and it appeared to be headed their way.

"We need to get out of here!" he shouted at Joshua and Jackson. "Hold on tight!" he yelled over his shoulder at Alison as he spun the four-wheeler around. Joshua and Jackson quickly followed suit. Maybe they could outrace the twister. It was their only hope.

Wyatt hit a bump in the pasture and the four-wheeler went airborne, sailing sideways across the field. Alison screamed and he felt her slipping off the seat, but her arms clamped down tighter around his waist, and somehow she held on as Wyatt clung to the handlebars. They landed with a thud but didn't even have time to breathe a sigh of relief. They had to keep moving forward.

By now, the roar of the Petree brothers' engine was almost totally drowned out by the ever-increasing wind. Wyatt felt as if a gigantic lion was angrily chasing them. He turned his head to look. The tornado had drawn closer. It was whipping along the countryside faster than the four-wheelers could go. Suddenly the cloud of dust that fanned out around the bottom of the funnel began to envelop them, making it difficult for Wyatt to see. A rock that had been picked up by the strong vortex hurtled past him, grazing his leg. It hit the front fender of his four-wheeler with a clang, leaving a deep dent.

The tornado hadn't reached them yet, but it'd become as dangerous as an exploding bomb. Its uncaring winds turned the ordinary rocks and branches that dotted the pasture into projectile missiles. Wyatt knew they needed to get as low to the ground as possible to avoid being hit.

Ahead of the whirling mist of kicked up dirt, he caught a glimpse of the creek in the shallow ravine that they'd passed through earlier, and he braked as hard as he could.

"What's wrong?" Jackson shouted as he and Joshua slowed down beside them. "We need to keep going!"

"We can't beat it! Make a run for the ravine and lie flat!" Wyatt shouted back. He jumped off the four-wheeler and grabbed Alison by the hand, dragging her along until she began to match his stride.

Once Wyatt reached the creek, he flung himself next to the water's edge and let go of Alison's hand. "Cover your head with your arms!" he barked.

Joshua and Jackson did the same, and the four lay in a row as the wind became more violent. Wyatt peeked sideways at Alison just as an old horseshoe struck the ground between them. They both flinched, but remained flattened against the earth.

Then Wyatt heard the dreaded rumble of the twister approaching. A frightened wail came from Joshua, who was stretched out on the other side of Wyatt.

Wyatt faced him. "Are you okay?" he shouted. He felt like they were in the middle of some war movie. Soldiers in a foxhole. But the enemy was Mother Nature.

Joshua nodded, his arms cradling his head. "I'm just scared," he yelled. "We're not going to make it."

Wyatt was scared, too, but he tried to calm his friend. "Hang on! It'll be over soon."

The tornado would be on top of them in a matter of seconds. It would batter them.

Fling them like rag dolls. *There's nothing to cling to*, Wyatt thought, *except for hope.*

It took a second to register, but the noise suddenly seemed to grow quieter instead of louder. The thundering roar was retreating and the gusting wind became less angry. Was it losing strength? Wyatt poked his head up. The dust seemed to be settling, so after a moment he leapt to his feet and scrambled up the side of the ravine. He expected to see a vanishing wisp of what once was. But that was not the sight that met him.

"No!" he shouted in disbelief. "It can't be!"

By this time Alison, Joshua, and Jackson had followed him, and the four kids stood frozen with a mixture of horror and relief. Beyond where they'd ditched their four-wheelers, the tornado loomed just as large, ominous, and awful as it had before. But it had changed course. It wasn't heading their way . . . it was careening straight for Wyatt's father.

His dad's truck was much closer than when they'd first noticed the tornado forming. *I bet he chased after us*, Wyatt thought. And now the tornado was barreling toward the white truck. He watched helplessly as the truck screeched to a stop, and began speeding backward.

Wyatt took a few steps forward, but Alison grabbed his arm. "It's too late. Oh, Uncle Ted!" she sobbed.

Wyatt put his arm around her and they both watched in horror as the tornado picked up the truck and tossed it like a toy, flipping it in the air and dropping it back to the ground in its wake.

# CHAPTER 6

Wyatt's heart leapt to his throat as he jumped on his four-wheeler. Alison slid on behind him. Without a word, Joshua and Jackson revved up their four-wheeler, too, and they were off, heading for the truck, which had finally come to rest.

Wyatt kept hoping he'd see a figure crawl out the side window. Anything that would signal his father was okay. But all was still around the truck as the tornado raged on in the distance.

Though it took less than five minutes to reach the crumpled, dented pickup, it was the longest ride of Wyatt's life. As soon as they were close enough, he flung himself off the four-wheeler in a mad dash to find his father. He should have been scared at what he might see, but his adrenaline was pumping and instinct took over. "Dad!" he yelled.

Wyatt dropped to his knees and peered through the broken window on the driver's side. Alison crouched beside him while Jackson and Joshua stood a short way behind.

"What are we going to do? What are we

going to do?" Joshua's voice rang out in a panic. "What if Mr. Anderson is dead?"

Alison turned to shush him. "Getting hysterical won't help anything. We need to stay calm!"

Mr. Anderson lay sprawled inside the truck. Everything was topsy-turvy. The bench seat and steering wheel hung over his body. And he wasn't moving.

"Dad! Dad!" Wyatt screamed. He reached through the shattered glass and touched his father's shoulder.

Mr. Anderson groaned and lifted his head. His forehead was bleeding and when he reached up to touch the spot, he grimaced. But soon he was smiling broadly. "Wyatt, thank God you are okay!" Then he noticed the others, who were staring at him with concern. "Y'all, too!" He pushed away some shards of glass from the window and struggled to scooch out. But before long, he stopped and grimaced again.

"What is it, Dad?" Wyatt asked.

"My ankle. It hurts. Worse than my head."

"Maybe you shouldn't move," Alison said.

"No. I'm fine." He tried again and this time managed to crawl out despite the pain. Wyatt and the others gathered around, helped him up, and supported him as he hobbled on one foot. Slowly, they inched their way around the broken glass and away from the smashed bits of truck.

"I'm still feelin' a little woozy," Mr. Anderson said as he promptly collapsed to the ground. The gash on his forehead trickled a steady stream of blood that soaked his shirt bright red.

The sight made Wyatt feel sick. Dizzy. Like he was going to pass out. "I'm not feelin' so hot either," he said.

"Why don't you sit down and put your

head between your knees," Alison suggested to her cousin.

Wyatt wanted to help his dad, but if he fainted, he wouldn't be any good to anyone at all. He did as he was told.

"Jackson — you're wearing an undershirt, right?" Alison asked. "Maybe you should take it off."

Jackson looked at her like she had lost her senses. He squinted in confusion. "What?"

"I was just thinking maybe I could use your undershirt to make a compress for Uncle Ted's wound," she explained. "You know, to stop the bleeding."

"Oh, okay." Jackson began taking off his shirt while Alison studied the gash on Mr. Anderson's forehead.

"You may need a few stitches," she told her uncle, "but we'll try to slow the bleeding until we can get you to a hospital. There's a bump, too. Do you think you got a concussion? You were unconscious, weren't you?"

"I don't know. I just remember the tornado turning back on me and the truck lifting off the ground. Then nothing until I heard Wyatt's voice."

Jackson handed his white T-shirt to Alison and she folded it into a thick square, pressing it against the gaping, bloodied gash.

"What can I do?" Joshua asked.

"Drag over the toolbox that was thrown from the back of the truck," Alison said.

"We can use it to prop Uncle Ted's leg up."
She took off her uncle's boot and rolled up
his jeans. "Looks puffy, but not too weird.
Hopcfully you didn't break any bones.
Keeping your foot raised will help keep it
from swelling too much for now," she said.

As Alison played nurse to her uncle,
Wyatt began to breathe easier and the
light-headed, queasy feeling faded. He felt
a rush of gratitude for his cousin. She
seemed to know what she was doing. He
lifted his head from his knees. "How did
you learn all this stuff?" he asked.

"What stuff?" she asked.

"First aid."

She shrugged like it was no big deal.
"Girl Scouts. I earned a badge."

"Did you see the first tornado, Dad?" Wyatt asked.

Mr. Anderson nodded. "I was busy mending the fence line and noticed a storm was brewing. Didn't think much of it and was trying to get as much done as I could before it hit. By the time I looked up from the fence line and actually saw the tornado, it looked like it was over our place. I was so worried about y'all. I was on my way back to the house to check on you when the second one touched down. How's everything at home?" he asked, concern lining his face. "Any damage?"

"Part of the barn roof is gone. Our front porch was totaled. And the garage is a mess," Wyatt told his father.

"Nothing that can't be repaired," his father said. He took the T-shirt compress from Alison and continued to press it against his head.

Wyatt was about to tell his father about Licorice running off, but before he could say anything, Mr. Anderson twisted his neck around and said, "I've lost my bearings. Now, which direction did the second twister go?"

Everyone had been so concerned with Wyatt's father that they'd forgotten the tornado might still be wreaking havoc on the countryside.

"Over there!" Joshua exclaimed.

The group stared off past a broken fence line. All the hard work Wyatt's father had done to repair it was gone in an instant when the tornado had carelessly ripped its posts from the ground. The fast-moving tornado was already miles away, its funnel still descended from the darkened sky, tracing the ground with a brown whirl-pool of dust.

"It looks like it's headed for our ranch," Jackson said.

# CHAPTER 7

Joshua, his eyes never leaving the tornado, put a hand on Mr. Anderson's shoulder. "Are you okay for now?" he asked.

"Sure," Mr. Anderson said. The trickle of blood from his head was beginning to cake and dry.

Before anyone could say or do anything, Joshua took off running for one of the four-wheelers. The younger of the Petree boys called over his shoulder, "I've got to check on Mom and Dad!"

"Wait!" Jackson yelled after him, but it was no use. Joshua had already started the motor and was off. Jackson shook his head in despair and rushed toward the other four-wheeler. "I've got to go after my brother," he told everyone.

"You go with Jackson," Alison urged Wyatt. "I'll stay here with Uncle Ted."

Once again, Wyatt felt grateful to have his cousin around. He didn't mind her silly pink ballet T-shirt anymore. Or her mushy, sappy way with Duncan. Or that she occasionally broke out in giggles. He never imagined she'd turn out to be someone he could count on. But she was. Now he could help his friends check on their family the way they just helped him check on his. His father was in good hands. He bolted after Jackson, not waiting to hear what his father would have to say about the matter.

Wyatt hopped on the already revved-up four-wheeler, and he and Jackson zipped off toward the funnel, chasing it in a race they could not win.

By the time the Petree ranch came into view, the twister was long gone, but it had made its powerful presence known. Jackson let out a whimper, and when Wyatt saw why, his jaw dropped. Joshua and Jackson lived in a large two-story house, but now it was missing most of its second floor.

As they sped closer, Wyatt gasped. Two navy-blue painted bed frames lay broken in the front yard. A brown bedspread hung, flapping, from a tree. Splintered beams that once held up the roof of the second floor lay scattered, like a large-scale version of pick-up sticks. Pink insulation dotted the landscape.

Wyatt was surprised to see Mr. Petree's truck parked by an outbuilding. Both appeared untouched, looking strangely out of place among the destruction. Once they were close enough, Jackson parked the four-wheeler next to the one Joshua had been riding.

Joshua stood nearby holding his head in his hands. He looked like he was about to crumple, but then he took a breath and, with a look of determination, stumbled forward toward the house.

Jackson grabbed his brother by the arm, steadying him. "It will be all right. Come on. We need to check for Mom and Dad in the storm cellar," he said.

Wyatt followed his friends to the rear of the house where they found something new to worry about. An enormous pile of debris from the second floor, including a heavy dresser drawer, covered the cellar doors.

"If they're down there, we can't reach them this way. We need to go through the house," Jackson said.

Wyatt ran to the front of the house along with his friends. He peeked into a broken window. The first floor was still standing, but everything was a mess. The family room, which Mrs. Petree usually kept clean and tidy, was strewn with upset furniture, papers, and books.

Joshua threw open the front door and rushed inside. "Mom! Dad!" he yelled.

"Wait!" Wyatt said. "Slow down! We need to be careful!"

Joshua ignored his warning, so Wyatt and Jackson had no choice but to follow him. Once they caught up to him inside the entry hall, they were met with an unsettling sight. The stairway that had once run up to the bedrooms now led to only a small bit of the second floor that still existed, and beyond that was open sky.

"Hey! I hear something up there!" Joshua said. "Maybe Mom and Dad are trapped!"

Before Wyatt could stop him, Joshua raced up the flight of stairs.

"Don't!" Jackson called after his brother. "The floor up there can't be stable!"

But Joshua was on a mission. He had to find his parents. It was as if he couldn't hear anything or anyone over the panicked voices inside his head.

Once again, Jackson and Wyatt started after him. But just as they dashed up the steps, the stairs groaned under their feet.

*Creak!* Wyatt felt the staircase shift. Joshua screamed. Instinctively, Wyatt reached out to grab on to the railing.

But it was no use.

The entire staircase gave way. Wyatt felt an awful lurch and suddenly he was falling . . . flailing . . . and crashing to the ground.

# CHAPTER 8

Wyatt's body slammed into the sharp edge of the stairs where they met the floor below. Before he could so much as blink, a large chunk of drywall fell on top of him. It took him a moment to register what had happened and to fill his lungs with air. His arm hurt, but he managed to push the drywall off and look around.

Jackson, lying only inches away, coughed

out a mouthful of dust and rubbed the back of his head, shaking loose a dusting of powder that coated his long dark hair.

Wyatt struggled to stand up on the pile of twisted wood that was once the staircase. His arm was scraped, and he would probably sport a couple of bruises in the days to come, but otherwise he seemed okay. "Where's Joshua?" he asked.

Jackson looked around in a wide-eyed panic. He began sifting like crazy through the debris next to him.

*Joshua was near the top*, Wyatt thought. That meant he had the farthest to fall! Wyatt glanced up . . . and noticed Joshua's familiar boots dangling from above. A pair of legs thrashed back and forth frantically.

They were attached to a torso and arms that clung to a banister spindle that still stubbornly remained on the second-floor landing.

"Joshua?" Wyatt asked.

"Who do you think! Get me down from here!"

Jackson couldn't help but laugh.

Wyatt grinned.

The two of them got into place on either side of the dangling legs. They steadied themselves on the uneven floor and reached their arms up. "Drop down, buddy, we got ya," Wyatt called.

"You sure?" Joshua asked nervously.

Wyatt touched his ankle. "Inch backward and it'll only be a short drop."

Joshua slowly slid himself until his balance shifted and he lost his grasp. Jackson and Wyatt helped break his fall, but they all landed in a heap.

Before Joshua could even joke about what "supportive" friends he had, they heard muffled noises from the rear of the house. Yelling and pounding.

"Mom! Dad!" Jackson sprang to his feet.

The three boys picked their way to the kitchen at the back of the house.

The ruckus was coming from the other

side of a door that led to the cellar. But they couldn't just open it. The Petrees' refrigerator had toppled over and blocked the door from being opened.

"Jackson! Joshua!" Wyatt heard Mr. Petree shout. "Is that you? Are you out there? Are you hurt?"

"I know I heard them," Mrs. Petree cried. "They were screaming. Something crashed. Oh, please let them be all right. Please, please, please . . ."

"Mom, it's us!" Joshua made his way closer to the door. "We're okay! How are you?"

"We're fine!" his mother answered.

"Just trapped," his father said. "Both the outside and inside doors won't budge."

The three boys gathered around the refrigerator.

"There's no way we can lift this thing," said Jackson. "What are we going to do?"

"We've got to try something," Joshua pleaded. "We've got to get them out!"

Wyatt knew how his friends must be feeling. Powerless. That's how he felt when he couldn't stop the tornado from hitting his dad's truck. "Why don't we push really hard and see if we can move it over."

After some straining, they were able to shove over the refrigerator just enough for the cellar door to swing open, and almost instantly Mr. and Mrs. Petree were rushing for their boys. Mrs. Petree hugged each one in turn, and then she hugged Wyatt, too. "We saw the tornado coming and made it to the cellar, but I was so worried about you. It was awful knowing you were miles away and there was nothing I could do!"

Mr. Petree looked around the kitchen at the destruction the tornado had wrought. Broken dishes. Furniture tossed about. Everything in shambles. "Oh, what a mess!" he said. "It sounded like the tornado hit us, but I was hoping the old house would be okay. Down in the cellar I had no idea . . ." His voice trailed off.

"Most of the second floor is gone," Jackson told his parents.

Mrs. Petree looked on the verge of tears, but she took a deep breath. "I am just so thankful we're all okay. I think I could take just about anything but losing you boys."

"How's your place?" Mr. Petree asked Wyatt.

"Better off than yours," Wyatt said. "Our house made it through. Our garage and barn weren't as lucky. But my dad was caught in an open field in his truck. The tornado tossed him around . . ." Wyatt's voice trembled a bit. "He's hurt — not badly — but he should probably go to the emergency room. His truck is totaled. My cousin, Alison, stayed with him while we came looking for you guys."

"Our truck looks okay, Dad. I saw it parked just like always. Not a dent," Jackson said. "Maybe you and Wyatt could go help Mr. Anderson?"

"Sure thing. I'd be happy to."

"What about your mother?" Mrs. Petree asked Wyatt.

"She was running errands in town. I'm hoping none of the tornadoes made it over there."

"Tornadoes?" Mrs. Petree asked. "You mean there was more than the one we saw?"

"There were two. At least that I know of," said Wyatt.

"Must have been a supercell storm," Mr. Petree said. He walked to a broken window and looked outside. A ripped curtain, which hung at a crooked angle, flapped in the gentle breeze.

The rest of the family crowded around. It looked like any ordinary day. So much so that Wyatt thought it was a little spooky.

# CHAPTER 9

Joshua and Jackson stayed behind with their mother to begin sorting through the wreckage. Wyatt and Mr. Petree jumped in his truck to head out for the pasture where Wyatt had left his father and Alison. When the truck came into view, its crumpled body overturned and damaged beyond repair, Mr. Petree gasped in amazement. "Your father — he was in that truck when the tornado hit?"

Wyatt nodded. In the distance, he saw Alison stand up and wave her arms over her head.

"There he is!" Wyatt shouted. His father lay on the ground beside Alison. As they drove closer, Mr. Anderson managed to lift his body into a sitting position and began waving as well. He must have been feeling at least a little okay.

Mr. Petree pulled up his truck next to them and hopped out. "You certainly are a lucky one," he said to his neighbor, shaking his head at the battered truck.

"Don't I know it," Mr. Anderson said. "How'd you folks fare?"

"We're okay, but the house isn't. The whole second story is gone."

"Sorry to hear it." Wyatt's dad shook his head in sympathy. "Anything we can do to help, just let us know."

"Thanks," Mr. Petree said. "But first things first. We need to get you to the emergency room." He knelt down. "Wyatt said that you may need stitches. And that your ankle is bothering you. Can you walk?"

Mr. Anderson waved him off. "The emergency room can wait. If my wife comes home from town and can't find anyone she'll be frantic. I tried calling, but the nearest cell tower must be down. If you can just drop us off at our place, I'll wait for her to come back and she can take me in."

As Mr. Petree helped lift Mr. Anderson into the back of the pickup truck, Wyatt couldn't help but worry about his mother. How many tornadoes could a supercell storm spawn? Could one have made it all the way to town?

Wyatt rode in the back with his father while Alison sat in front with Mr. Petree for the bumpy trip through the fields back home. Mr. Anderson grimaced from time to time with the jostling his injured ankle took, but he also smiled reassuringly at Wyatt and patted his knee. Wyatt should have been the one comforting his dad, but he was still too upset about the events of the day.

"Licorice is gone. He crashed through

his stall door and bolted right before the tornado hit the barn." Wyatt moped.

"He's a smart horse. And fast," his father said. "He'll find his way back."

Still, Wyatt's thoughts went to dark places. Not only about Licorice, but about his mother, too. He remembered watching the news last year when a tornado wiped out an entire Kansas neighborhood. Several hundred houses were flattened. The ranch where he lived sat in mostly open country, but there was a lot more going on in town. What if the grocery store was obliterated?

As they approached the house, Wyatt practically strained his eyes looking for his mother's car. It was nowhere to be seen. She wasn't home yet. But by the time they began helping his father out of the back of Mr. Petree's truck, her green SUV was speeding down the gravel driveway toward them, leaving a trail of dust. She came to an abrupt stop and leapt out of the driver's-side door. "You're okay!" she panted. "Everyone in town was talking about the tornadoes!" Wyatt thought his mom looked relieved to see them, but when she took in the missing barn roof and the busted garage and the decimated front porch, her expression changed to one of stunned realization. And when she noticed the dried blood on her husband's forehead and saw how Mr. Pctree was supporting him, it turned to something worse. "Oh, Ted!" she exclaimed.

"I'm fine, Beth. It's nothing to be worried about," Wyatt's father reassured her. "Alison here was a great nurse, and the doctors at the emergency room will be able to patch me right up. But first I want to tour the property. Make sure none of the cattle are hurt and see what's what."

"Are you sure that's a good idea, Uncle Ted?" Alison asked. "You have to get that cut cleaned or it'll get infected."

"Yes, Doctor Alison," he said with a wink. "I promise I'll go soon. Wyatt, take care of your cousin. I'll keep a lookout for Licorice." With that, Wyatt's parents jumped into the SUV and headed out to check the damage. And with everything at the Andersons' under control, Mr. Petree decided to head back to help his own family with the long clean-up process ahead.

Alison and Wyatt walked to the barn to get a better look at how the horses and goats had fared.

"Maybe Licorice has already come back," Alison said. Wyatt hoped she was right, that he'd see Licorice in his stall, like nothing had ever happened.

But the stall with the busted door was empty. One by one, Alison and Wyatt gave the animals a good going-over. Molasses had a cut on his flank that looked raw, so Alison helped him disinfect and bandage it. "We'll get the vet out here to check on him tomorrow," Wyatt said. "He'll probably need a round of antibiotics, but I imagine he'll be fine."

"Hey, where's Duncan?" Alison asked.

Wyatt looked around. "He isn't with the goats?"

"Nope." Alison frowned. "I haven't seen him at all since we came back. Have you?"

Wyatt shook his head. He ran outside with Alison and they both called for him. No big white shaggy creature came.

"Maybe he went looking for us," Alison said. She started to pace back and forth nervously. "What if he got caught in the second tornado?"

Wyatt tried to remain calm but felt a sudden, painful rush of emotion now that the adrenaline of the immediate aftermath of the tornadoes was over. He loved Licorice. He loved Duncan. He couldn't imagine life on the ranch without them!

Next thing he knew, Alison let out a squeal and pointed.

There was Duncan slowly making his way toward the barn, leading the way as a limping Licorice trailed behind him.

Every once in a while the dog would stop and wait for the horse to catch up with him.

*Good old Duncan found Licorice for me,* Wyatt thought. He was doing his job, taking care of his animals.

Alison ran to greet Duncan and smothered him with hugs and kisses. Wyatt raced for Licorice and wrapped his arms around the horse's neck. Licorice's long mane tickled his nose. He checked Licorice's leg. The vet would have another patient to see in the morning.

The cousins walked the animals the rest of the way to the barn.

"I'm going to miss Duncan like crazy when I go back to New York," Alison said. She paused a moment and then said, "And I'm going to miss you, too, Wyatt."

Wyatt thought for a moment. Alison was smart. And tougher than she looked. And she cared about his animals as much as he did. She'd turned out to be all right. "I guess I'll miss you, too," he said with a laugh. He hadn't thought it possible, but he really and truly meant it.

# CHAPTER 10

Wyatt saw a cluster of skyscrapers all crowded together out the plane window. The scenery was so different than the miles and miles of grassy fields back home. Soon the plane would circle and land, dropping him off among the steel and concrete giants.

His mother nudged him and flashed a smile. "Won't be long," she said. She'd be

spending a few days with her sister's family before flying back to the ranch, leaving Wyatt for an extended stay in the big city. "Are you excited?" she asked. "You've been rather quiet."

Wyatt nodded and grinned. "Don't worry. I'm excited. I was just thinking about when Alison came to visit us in Oklahoma." The harsh August sunlight streamed in through the small window, making Wyatt squint. The two tornadoes that'd shook up his world in early June already seemed like distant history. Besides the damage to their property and to the Petrees', three other homes and at least two barns had been destroyed. Luckily their county wasn't heavily populated. Wyatt's family had also lost six cows when the tornadoes struck, but considering how large a herd they had, it didn't damage the family business too much, though he was sad for the loss. Joshua, Jackson, and their parents had ended up staying with the Andersons through mid-July, until the repairs to their home made it livable. It'd been crowded, especially in the evenings when everyone gathered after a hard day's work, but it'd been sort of fun, too, to have a boisterous full house. Especially since he was an only child.

"It'll be so nice to see Alison again," his mother said. "I sure got attached to having that girl around for a while!"

His mother was right. It would be nice to see Alison again, Wyatt thought. He couldn't believe how close he'd gotten to his cousin in the two weeks she'd stayed at the ranch. They'd worked side by side, helping with cleanup and taking care of the many animals on the ranch. But his parents made sure they also had time just to hang out and have fun. It turned out he'd been right about her. She was a totally girly girl. But she was a hard worker, too. And she'd even managed to beat him at

*FreakFighters.* He'd almost gotten teary-eyed when she'd had to say good-bye but managed not to make a fool of himself. And he wasn't the only one who missed her. Jackson and Joshua were sad to see her go, too. Even Duncan had moped around for days after she left. Wyatt remembered Alison wistfully mentioning wanting to smuggle Duncan home in her suitcase. If the laws of physics had allowed, she probably would have!

Wyatt dragged his carry-on bag behind him and peered into the waiting crowd at the airport. Suddenly he spied a familiar face. A dark-haired girl waving wildly and jumping up and down. She bolted from her mother and rushed over to him. "You're here! You're here! I can't believe you're here!"

Wyatt laughed. "Yeah, I'm here. I'm not a mirage. At least I don't think I am."

Alison jokingly poked him, as if checking to make sure. "Yep. You're real all right! How is Licorice? And Duncan?" she asked Wyatt.

"Licorice's leg is back to normal. No more limping. And I even started ramping him back up for barrel racing a few weeks ago. He's as fast as ever. Duncan is keeping order in the barn, as usual." Wyatt grinned. "After you left I was half afraid he would go off looking for you!"

"Aw, I still miss the big guy," Alison said. "Hey, what do you want to see first?

Dinosaurs at the Museum of Natural History or mummies at the Metropolitan Museum of Art?"

It was a hard decision, both sounded cool. "Mummies," Wyatt finally decided.

"But first we have to get you settled in at our new apartment," Alison said. "Did my mom tell you guys that we moved last month? The new apartment isn't that far from our old place. And there is one really super great thing about it. It's a surprise. I can't wait to show you!"

On the taxi drive to the apartment, Alison talked about all of the plans she'd made for his stay. A funny Broadway show with lots of action, a trip to Ellis Island and the Statue of Liberty, and a visit to Times

Square. Wyatt remembered how, at the beginning of summer, he imagined being cooped up all day with nothing to do. Boy, did he have it wrong — it sounded like Alison was going to keep him very busy!

Before long the taxi ride was over and Alison's mother was fishing for her keys to unlock the door to their new apartment.

"So time for the surprise?" Wyatt asked.

"Just wait," Alison said.

The door swung open and a tiny white dog bounded toward Wyatt! A scruffy mutt that looked like a miniature version of Duncan.

"Our new apartment allows pets! I finally have a dog!" Alison shouted. She scooped the puppy up and cuddled him. "His name is Twister. We got him from the animal shelter a few weeks ago." She put the dog down, and soon Twister was zipping and circling around them like a windup toy. "I named him Twister because he reminds me of a little tornado when he gets excited. And also because, well, you know . . . everything that we went through together."

Wyatt was glad his cousin finally had a pet. As much as she loved animals she deserved to have one. But even though she now had a dog of her own, Wyatt hoped Alison would come back to the ranch next summer. He had to admit, despite his initial feelings, the cousin swap idea his mother and aunt came up with ended up being pretty cool.

"Here, boy," Wyatt called. The little dog ran toward him, tail wagging. Twister jumped and barked and spun around until Wyatt couldn't help but laugh. And when he finally slowed down, Wyatt patted his head. "Nice to meet you, Twister," he said. "No offense, but I hope you're the very last Twister I'll ever meet!"

"I'll second that!" Alison knelt down to pet Twister, too, and she and Wyatt exchanged a look that didn't need words. They'd shared moments of sheer terror together. But they'd survived.

"So are you ready to go face those mummies?" Alison asked.

"Sure," Wyatt said.

In fact, he couldn't wait!

# More About
# TORNADOES

Tornadoes form from thunderstorms. Much remains a mystery about how tornadoes are created, but it involves warm, moist air colliding with cool dry air. This can cause the air to rotate and twist into a funnel or rope shape.

Tornadoes have been recorded on every continent except for Antarctica. The United States averages over 1,200 tornadoes every year, more than any other country. Most happen in a geographic region called Tornado Alley, a flat stretch of land between Texas and North Dakota.

Most tornadoes go less than 100 miles per hour and only travel a few miles before vanishing. But extreme tornadoes can reach speeds of more than 300 miles per hour and can travel over 100 miles.

One of the longest and deadliest tornadoes on record, the Tri-State Tornado of 1925, traveled for 3.5 hours through parts of Missouri, Illinois, and Indiana. It left a path of destruction more than 219 miles long.

A tornado in Kansas once plucked the feathers right off some chickens. In Oklahoma, a tornado picked up and carried a small herd of cattle before finally depositing them in another part of the countryside, uninjured. Waterspouts, which are tornadoes that form over bodies of water, have been known to rain fish and frogs!

The word *tornado* was banned from use in weather forecasting from 1887 to 1952. At the time, technology could not predict where or when a tornado would hit and little was understood about how they formed, so it was thought that using the word would spread unnecessary panic.

Fortunately we now know a lot more about tornadoes. Meteorologists can predict if conditions are favorable for their formation. The National Weather Service (NWS) issues tornado forecasts using real-time weather observations from many different technologies including satellites, weather stations, balloon packages, airplanes, wind profilers, and radar.

When meteorologists issue a Tornado Watch, it means the conditions are right for tornado formation. Stay tuned to the radio or television news for more information. A Tornado Warning means a tornado has actually been sighted, so you should seek shelter immediately. If there is a Tornado Warning in your area, there are some things you can do to help keep yourself safe:

• Go to an underground storm shelter or to a basement and protect yourself by crawling under something sturdy, like a table. Covering yourself with a mattress can also protect you from falling debris.

• In a home or building without an underground shelter or basement, stay on the first floor in a centrally located room without windows such as a bathroom, closet, or hallway, or underneath a stairwell. Crouch down low, facedown, and put your hands over your head. Place something over you for protection if possible.

• If you are outdoors without nearby shelter, seek low ground and lie flat, facedown. Protect the back of your head with your arms. Get as far away from trees and cars as you can, as tornado winds can lift them and blow them around in unpredictable ways.

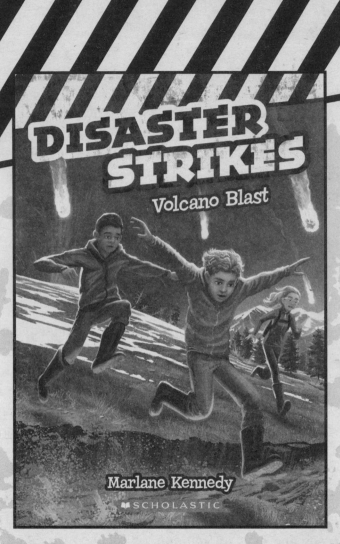

Ready for another thrilling adventure?
Read on for a sneak peek at
VOLCANO BLAST...

Noah looked toward the summit of the volcano. It seemed peaceful under the blue skies, but he turned toward his sister for reassurance anyway. "It's not going to erupt, is it?" he yelled over the roar.

"I don't know, but I'm not sticking around to find out!" Emma yelled back. "We need to head back to the boat."

"I'm with you. This is freaking me out. I've never heard anything like it before!" Alex said.

They scrambled down the mountainside as best they could, the scary-loud rumbling sound chasing after them. But it was slowgoing. Painfully slow. Running down the uneven, sloping ground was next to impossible.

"Dad said this volcano might not blow for a hundred years," Noah called out to the other two in ragged huffs. "Maybe thousands."

"In other words, it's totally unpredictable!" Emma barked back. "We can't take any chances. There's no telling how dangerous it may be!"

But Noah wasn't listening anymore. Because just then he lost his footing on the rough terrain, fell to the ground, and slid down the slope feetfirst. His body twisted, and his stomach scraped the ground as he skidded farther down the slope. Rocks ripped at his jacket and he clawed at everything he could to stop his momentum.

Finally he slowed enough to struggle

back to his feet. He looked up the mountainside to where they'd just come from and stood paralyzed for a moment, not quite believing what he saw. "Guys! Stop! Look!" he screamed.

A deep vertical crack in the earth was cleaving the ground before his eyes. Steam and smoke sprang from the crack, which expanded quickly, snaking down toward them.

The other two stopped in their tracks and turned to see what Noah was screaming about.

"It's a fissure," Emma shouted. "And it'll make its way to us in a matter of seconds. We need to keep going! It could start spewing lava!"

As they hustled toward the shoreline, which still seemed impossibly far off, Noah kept glancing behind them. The fissure seemed to be catching up. It was spreading faster than they could run.

*Maybe we should be running sideways to escape it,* Noah thought. But by that time, they'd reached a dip in the slope that suddenly deepened and narrowed — a natural crevice that had formed years ago. They'd have to climb up a steep embankment to go sideways, which would take too much time.

"Hurry!" Alex screamed at the twins.

But Noah couldn't help craning his neck to look at the rift again. Lava was already spewing into the air where it'd first opened up. And just feet behind them, the earth continued to crack open. "It caught us! Jump to the side! Jump to the side!" Noah bellowed.

Alex and Emma jumped to the right. Noah jumped to the left. In an instant they were separated by the fissure, which had split the earth between them.

# DO YOU HAVE WHAT IT TAKES TO SURVIVE?

READ THEM ALL, THEN TAKE THE QUIZ TO TEST YOUR
SURVIVAL SKILLS AT WWW.SCHOLASTIC.COM/ISURVIVED.